Christmas 1977

For John—

I do believe I sometimes get downright balmy when I'm book-buying. Anyhow, I couldn't resist this, & do hope you yyk it as much as I did! :)

Mom

AB TO ZOGG

*A Lexicon for Science-Fiction
and Fantasy Readers*

BOOKS BY EVE MERRIAM

*Catch a Little Rhyme
There Is No Rhyme for Silver
Finding a Poem
It Doesn't Always Have to Rhyme
Out Loud
Rainbow Writing
Ab to Zogg*

AB to ZOGG

A Lexicon
for Science-Fiction and
Fantasy Readers

by Eve Merriam

DRAWINGS BY AL LORENZ

Atheneum 1977 *New York*

LIBRARY OF CONGRESS CATALOGING IN PUBLICATION DATA

Merriam, Eve   Ab to zogg.

SUMMARY: A spoof of science fiction and fantasy
through a brief dictionary of new—but recognizable—
words and phrases.
1. Science fiction—Anecdotes, facetiae, satire, etc.
[1. Science fiction—Anecdotes, facetiae, satire, etc.]
I. Lorenz, Albert   II. Title.
PS3525.E639A63   818'.5'407   77–1629
ISBN 0–689–30591–5

Copyright © 1977 by Eve Merriam
Published simultaneously in Canada by McClelland & Stewart, Ltd.
Printed in the United States of America by
The Murray Printing Company, Forge Village, Massachusetts
Bound by A. Horowitz & Son / Bookbinders
Fairfield, New Jersey
Designed by Mary M. Ahern
First Edition

AB TO ZOGG

*A Lexicon for Science-Fiction
and Fantasy Readers*

ANTANA

A

AB(AB) [From the early Ablative, initially a being from above; variants Abo, Abot, Aboba.]
The abominable Abonaut, able to fly through every zone in space, encumbered by naught save its own featherfurfin weight.

Antana (an-TA-na) [Old Frankish *anta*, below + *ta*, small.]
Queen of intelligent insect life ruling under the Sahara.

Armondo (ar-MON-do) [Middle Sextant noun, singularly plural.]
The bellicose fleet of the Viking,

3

Armond the Armorer. Having successfully sunk the tankards and capstans of Vestvaard the Vincible, the victors capsized on New Founderland, their vizors and brigandines entangling in the houppelands.

Audorio (au-DOR-i-O) [From the late Vorse *audin,* to send forth + *ri,* again.]
The great listening room where the All-Highest Ear gives commands in the deafening realm of Rodio.

B

Bandura waves (ban-DU-ra wayvz) [Modern Optical *bani,* to blot out + *duran,* appear.]
The illusion that black is white and vice-versa, engendered most clearly on the Zebu Plain inhabited principally by tribes of running zebras.

BBBR

BBBR (b-b-BR; also b-B-br; rarely B-b-br) [Pre-Icelandic construction.] Floating polar mass beyond the Antarctic. Foliage on BBBR consists of bbbracken, underbbbrsk, and frozen bbbrgers from the first expeditionary fossil force.

Binn (binn) See TERRAGLOBINN.

Bioffeneback (by-off-ENE-back) [Late middle Aromic *bioffener*, frequent + base of *feen*, ground.] Pulsing signals emanating from the giant cup-shaped telescopes atop Mount Moka.

C

Cape Cauldroon (Cape Cawl-DROON)

The outermost kettle of land that must be encompassed before anyone can enter the Capillary Ancillestial Promontory of Existence; also, the enveloping fog that covers every attempt to draw near.

Cheen (cheen) [From the Cappek *ch*, complaint or crying out, therefore alive + the suffix *een*, corruption of *ayn*, i.e. own or one.]

A species of humanoid with metallic flesh and wheeled limbs.

Cob o' my cob (cob o' my COB)

[Anggel-Flaxxon *cobo*, to stalk;

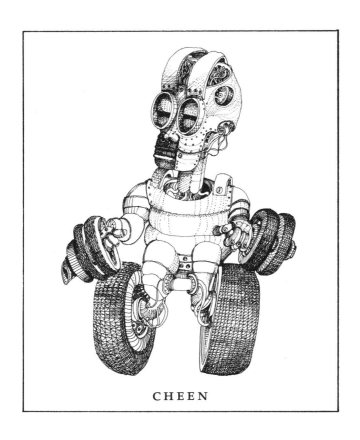

CHEEN

perhaps also from the Indo-Brackish *omy*, belonging to.]

The ultimate gleaning to be plucked from the overweaning maize crop before the silken-tasseled tresses of the Princess Kerenella can be freed from the omnivorous thorn thicket.

D

Desaulteining process (dee-sawl-TEEN-ing PRAH-sess)

Method by which brine deposits are brought up from the marine floor by pumping fresh air into the wave troughs; named after Daniele De Saulteine, an intimate of François Jules, who first vernerized the system.

Dewdaps (DOO-daps) [Middle Erse *diuda*, a joyful stomping dance + base of *ppps*, a sibilant afterthought.]

The merry wee goldwishers who dwell under the falls of the rushing glen. Contrary to popular belief, it does not bring shining happiness to toss them a coin; they merely make off with it after splashing the giver and have sometimes been known to swarm up from the falls in a greedy flock whence, with a rapid siffling Wishtawee!! (see FLOCKNOTE) they snatch up the entire contents of peregrines' purses.

Doog (doog) [Reverse Echoic.]
Four-eyed beast guarding the ooter gates of Oorioon; each eye keeping a successive six-hour alert out of the total quotidian watch.

D O O G

E

Eldron tablets (EL-dron TAB-lets) [Eldronian origin moot.]

The pre-Hammurabi Code of Ethics inscribed on sandalwood and adhered to by all citizens, citizanissaries, and citizorians as well as the freed serifs or meers. Upon the sacking of the city-state by sandalized vandals, the tablets were hidden in a fen of eldron-root, but the Effluvial Flude inundated the territory so deeply that the tablets became bloated and the inscriptions could no longer be deciphered.

Endra (EN-drah)

In the Anglo-Harold legend, they are the circle people, never-ending in their quest to conquer the darkness of Begon.

Excalibra (ex-CAL-ib-rah) [From

the Latinate *excaliber,* out of the book of california.]

Missing mate to the sword raised by our Lady of Shallott, still sought at the extensive Calburry archeological diggings where a portion of the halcyon appears to have been unearthed.

F

Falofola (fa-LO-fa-LAH) [Post-Aprillic *falof,* to strew + *faloa,* a ground cover.]

Flowering meadow-streets in the kingdom of Goldenore where every month is May.

Farenheitelburg front (fahr-en-HITE-el-buhrg FRUHNT)

The first law of tempodynamics, that as a zeppolone approaches a jet stream, it must condense or collapse.

11

Fellox (FELL-OX) [Etymythogical *fello*, an Ur-companion + *x*, sign of the uni-horned algebrach.]

The shod bare-hooved beast sacred to the goddess Oxymora. On shrine days the beast was baked, together with rosemary and myrtle garlands, into a kiln-cake to be eaten only by the chief altar attendants.

FELLOX

Flocknote (FLOK-noht)

Concerning a flock of dewdaps, the cry of *Wishtawee!* in daemonic dialect can be roughly translated as agitato, pronto, tempus fugit, vite alors.

Fragrancia   (fray-GRAN-see-ah) [Middle Italic.]

The *eternal* perfumed breeze that *wafts* over the *marble* bed of the leontine lovers, "Brother" Fra and "Sister" Grancia, who *petrified* themselves because they *believed* they were *siblings*, although *after* their stony demise Frio Patermoster discovered that their families were *in* actuality *total* strangers unto one *another*.

G

Ganymores (gan-im-OR-eez) Medieval Doric *beganner*, to start up + *gemorris*, a dance on one's knees.]

GANYMORES

The partially-dwarfed, quarter-immortal denizens of the land of Lumi, perisphere of perpetual twilight dawn.

Gerdule (gerd-YULE) [Great Norman akin to Scottish *gerra-gerra*,

14

very + base of *dul,* the least.]
The smallest coin in the realm of San, used as payment for armaments. "War is not worth two gerdules": San the Serene, Keeper of the Peace.

Gestote (jes-TOTE) [Variant pronun. jez-TOE-tee.]
Somatification theory of unified mind-body (soma) practice, gestated and carried on board the blastoff mission to Beelzebub's Galaxy by Lister B. Gezt, founder of the treble SSSence that with Soma, Summa, Sauna "the highest sum of body-heat furnaces the mind."

H

Hadronium (Hay-DRO-nee-yum)
Element formed by the interaction of an adronium atom with H.

HOVVERS

Hershebehemoth (her-she-BEE-he-muth)

In the Attick Book of Hershe-behemoth, *prima inter pares* of the

16

nine supreme muses, the sole begetter of earth, sea, sky, mountains, valleys, sun, moon and stars, while the eight remaining feminine deities reign over the interstices.

Hoberry (HO-beh-ree) [Botan; genus arborus; Rainian base may be *bha*—, gleam, shine.]
Bright red fruit of the hoberry tree; entirely edible, leaving no litter of rind, pit, stem or seeds. Blooms on holidays and private happiness days.

Hovvers (HUH-verz) [C.f. adj. *hovverian;* verb *to hovv and hovv not;* adv. *hovverly.*]
Half-souls who inhabit a zone midway between the mushroom caps and the sequoia tops. They glide silently as they sip of the humming mintsuckle and then float, seemingly motionless in air, as they chew

17

the mintsuckle stamen into slender balls and then stretch the delicate threads into nets for their hammock hums.

I

Illim (ILL-im) [From the Elegaic, "Speak no Ill of im."]
The once-great kingdom of the ancient Trepans, now a ruined archipelago, its abandoned arches and pelagos rusted by eight thousand centuries of ceaseless rainfall.

ILLIM

Ingulbury (IN-gull-burr-ee) [Botan; genus nixarborus.]
The false hoberry tree, planted by Mernil the Vain. Fruit is brilliant red until plucked, then turns bilious green.

J

Jample (JAM-pull) [Portmanteau; from the inventor Janus Emple, distinguished emplarian and janis-susitator.]
Post-biotic wimple used as a shield against rays re-emanating from fobworks.

Jocunda (YO-kun-dah; less often, yo-KUN-dah) [Vulgate; the ignis luciferis, perh. derived from *yokoo*, to burn or scorch, as a flambeau.]
Medieval marzipan for toasting wenches.

JAMPLE

Jyk (JYK) [Origin lost in jykquykuity.]
All-purpose word used by natives of the planet Jykon. Greetings, jyk. I jyk you. He is wearing his only jyk. No jyking allowed except at appointed jyks. Etjykera.

20

K

Kamordor (KA-mor-dor) [Gothic arch.; akin to Old Vaultic.]
In the kingdom of Kamordor, the eponymous room without a doorknob, which no mortal is permitted to enter.

Kurtt the Abrupt (KOORT th'ab-RUPPED) [Dates uncertain; possibly 8½–8¾.]
Wearer of the King's curtail for a brief interregnum between Languor the Longue-Tongued and Dalliance the Attenuate.

L

Lak (LAHK) [Suhthrun Colloq.; prob. arose from *myteelakka*, synonym.]
Red-naped Florrist monster that

LAK

lacks more lustrous description. Although claimed by some sighters to be a flying biped, by others a walking porpoise, and by still others a dish running away with a spoon, according to official Lak-listers, no real lak ness exists.

Lillizizz (LILL-ee-zizz) [See also *lillizizzor*, shears; also *lizzililli*, Elizabethan royal flower.]
Transistorized Tinytown whose mini-habitants operate on a form of energy emitted by ballpoint clicks.

Lingamoten (LING-a-MO-ten) [Old Vorse; *lingggen*, a pivot + *muuuter*, to scale a horned hide.]
Mountain of mountains, atop which stands the diamond castle Rhinestein with its revolving turreted tower that sends out rainbow rays to dazzle and delay all earthling climbers who venture beyond the barbican.

M

Maypolemes (may-po-LEE-mess) [Derived from the local dialects, since split, of the Magno-Mapes and Polandic-Olemes.]

23

One of the legends of the Book of Budenblume, namely, that on the first of Mapes, once every poleme, three Maypoles become capable of cognitive acts.

Mog (MAHH-g) [Abbrev. from Mogrog; after the Valhallian *mog-runewald*, wooden beaker or dripper. Now rare.]
A magic potion, compounded of cinnamoon and nightmeg.

Myushsludgkola (my-ush-SLUJ-kuh-la) [From the Serb *myush*, to mish or mosh + base of *slujakla*, a toast to long life.]
Soil environment, developed by a laboratory team of East-West ethnicians, that grows its own garbage and then converts it into edible sluice.

N

Nangle (NANG-uhl) [Nangolian, from *nangler*, to locate or ascertain, arrived at from the six acronymic points of the compass: Nang, Ast, Nang-by-Ast, Glar, Louth, and Estus.]
An identification ring worn upon the sixth finger by the parasextons of the satellite Sixtus.

Nawturex (naw-TOO-reks) [Ozic configuration, from *tornatur*, a great wind + base of *rexus*, hollow-hearted.]
Building materials of Bantambaumland, obtained from sawdust left by damming beavers along yellow brick roads.

Naytwanaytwa (NAY-twa-nay-TWA) See *Twatwa*.

NODDO

Noddo (NAH-DOUGH)
The dormant volcano-god.

Noddonoddonoddonoddo
(NAH-DOUGH-NAH-DOUGH-
NAH-DOUGH-NAH-DOUGH)
Great-grandson of the dormant vol-
cano-god.

26

O

Ogrimony (O-grih-MO-nee) [Middle Thesaurian, comp. with *matri, patri, acri, cere.*]

The desperate plight of somnolescent maidens who, wandering in the chimerical state of Og, are seized by their braids and bonded to stertorious ogres.

Omagma (o-MAG-ma) [Past future participle of *omagmos,* to divine.]

The perfect pyramid, forever under construction, never concluded.

Othon (O-thon) [From the Knothic; originally *othong,* to tie on.]

Initiation ceremony in Kinter where the newborn don their winged feet.

P

Paramax effect (PAR-a-max eff-ECHT)

That where the parameters of earth and the planet Xi converge, all boundary lines are maximized into parallels.

Poryphels (PORE-iff-ells) [L. *portio, portionis,* a portion + Gk. *phyllon,* a leaf.]

Harvested every quadrennial, the seeds can be crushed to kill serpents or flavor soup, and the berries made into a juice that, when thrown into the eyes of the beloved, can blind to all others.

Punj (PUNJ) [Variants are *punge, jnup, upng.*]

Creeping furze that covers the elders of lower Gorseland.

Q

Qattar (KAT-tar; rarely quat-TAR.)
[Gk. *kithara*; Australian, *qantas.*]
One-and-a-half stringed instrument
played by shepherds in the labor-
nian groves of Nigh.

?Quent? (KWENT)
The question that has no answer,
that yet needs must be asked con-
tinuously during the dimorphic fes-
tival of St. Quentin the Quarrier.

R

Rabot (RAY-bott) [From the Walloon
rabbett, young of the cony; also
Sanskrit *rabhas*, violence, force.]
Back in twenty-first century America, a species of rabbit that crossbred
with copying machines. In the

R A B O T

worldwide famine that followed the unwinning of the war against the Rabots, the last ream of carbon paper was consumed and history returned to its original oral tradition.

Ritipox (RIH-tih-poks) [Combining form from Late Culinarian *riti*, a cracker + *pox*, soy crumbs.]
High-protein grain used as feed for cattle and mulch for lasers.

Rogisigor (ro-GISS-ih-gore) [Past participle of the Palindromic.]
The backward country where one runs to catch up to what went before.

S

Seavelt (SEE-VELLT) [Akin to Dutch *zee;* also Scand. *sae.*]
Phosphorescence thrown up at high tide on the beaches of Veltira, sunken island in the central lunar crater system.

Seglunda (seh-GLUHN-dah) [From the old Flaxxen *seggelens-gulge,* a spool of thread.]
Garment of the Garbs, a singleton dhoti embroidered with such fine knots that the wearer becomes invisible.

SEGLUNDA

Straking (STRAY-KING) [Related to *straker, strakarama, strakingdome.*] Astrolabic power of planetarians on the asteroid Stele to phenomonize into meteoric marathons.

32

T

Terraglobin   (terr-ah-GLO-binn)
[Lat. *terranum, terrenum, terracea,* to
step up; also Fr. *tirer,* to draw or pull;
and Heb. *teraph, teraphim,* small
idol.]
In Pookish fairy tales, a sprite of
shimmering diaphinity who can
girdle the earth in a binn (thou-
sand-footed leap).

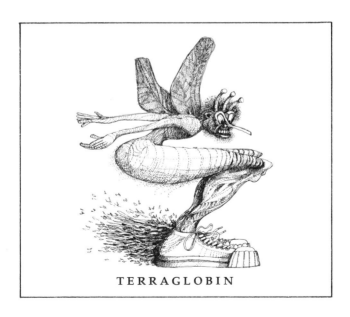

T E R R A G L O B I N

Triskan (TRISS-KAN)

Abbreviated name for Triskai-dekophilip, thirteenth son of Triskano the Thirteenth, capable of downing thirteen by thirteen in a flagon's fell.

Tropedarians (tro-peh-DAY-ree-anz) [From Muddle English *deierie*, a place where milk and cream are kept, also a personal notebook.]

TWATWA

In the Tropic of Trope, a race of vegetables subsisting on meatless munches and clotted whey-smacks.

Twatwa (TWA-twa) [Old Kiltish *twair* or *twain*, a paired vehicle.]
The double-tailed deer of the Dune Tundra, considered a sign of good fortune when one crosses the path of one, and a curse (NAYTWA-NAYTWA!!) upon any one who hunts one down.

U

Unicone (EWE-nik-ohn) [Origin and destination lost.]
Seared model for the uni-engined rocket, failed mode of flying carpet transport.

Unthunathule (un-THOO-na-thool) [Elderic *thunor*, also *thunun-*

derr, loud noise.] Paradisical playground beneath the forest floor, out of reach of Poluto the Black Sun and Terra the Night Mare, where childhood lasts an undread years.

Urburs (UR-berz) [From the Urbish, *urbum, urbanum*, place, placemat.] The bird people who live in square nests and feed by snapping leather pouches into a central head hole.

URBURS

V

Veddern (veh-DERN) [Ancient and modern Veddic, *edder-vedder*, a mix-up.]

Feast of the metabolic spirits on Veddermass Eve when female and male ions exchange pulses.

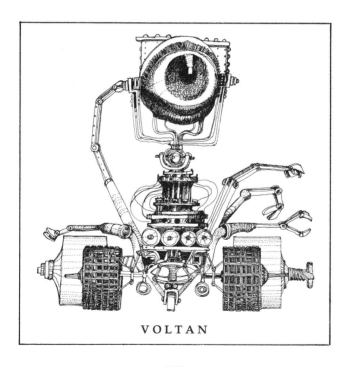

VOLTAN

37

Veilluris (vile-LOO-riss)

Faintly silverine shadow cast by the howling of Auld Rimer the Foxed between the dialect hours of ha' a'ter an' pass'd o'er.

Voltan (VOHL-tan) [See also Revoltan and Revolver.]

The battery-driven god whose electric eye powers the sun and is at ohm with all Parnassus.

W

Whhh (   ) [   ]

Broadcasting system on the silent planet Psye.

Wockups (WAH-CUPS) [Ancient Kupse, *wah*, to heave, haul.]

The twelve giant grimstones which,

in the weightless atmosphere of Wock, can be lifted by a fingerling.

Wy (WY) [From the Querian *wyzzit,* a redoubtable quest to shun.]
The metamorphic river that winds from Synechdoche to Simile as it leads on and on past the reverberating caves into the analagous springs of Aska.

X

XIVLCMXXXVILXVM (ick-VIL-sim-ICKS-vil-ICKS-vim)
Reincarnated Roman gladiator whose quarked tunic conceals deadly microwaves and whose name none dare pronounce aloud.

Xtrk (ick-STRIK) [Ixitonian, *xtr,* addition, addenda, passe-allee.]
Nuclearized passageway that, if not

XIVLCMXXXVILXVM

kept devoid of vowels, can exude a
fatal exeunt.

Y

Ydred (EE-dred) [ydates yunclyr.]
Ydred the Red (Claimant of Deeds)
and Ydred the Ded (Willer of Deeds)

both descended from Dred the Naught, but the true lineage remains in doubt, since which is the steptoe son and which the stepheel has never been resolved, due to Nurse Which's implanting of the royal dredneedle upon Ydred the Thred.

YDRED

Yffggtt (YIFF-git) [Memorian, *yofer*, bring back + *gititt*, recall.] Free-falling state of oblivion where all can be expunged from consciousness save the treble clef.

Yubble (yuh-bull) [Derived from the Fulleric, *ubbubb*, a bubbleless dome.] All that remains of the skyjacked planet after the automatic pilot has been accidentally unplugged.

Z

Zoadaster (zo-a-DAS-terr) [Lunitarian, *zodec*, a das master.] The followers of Zoadaster are neither a becoming nor an ungoing sect; their standard, a cross aslant (in the form of a cross a-slant) may be carried only by those members born at the cusp of the Zoadaster sign,

ZOADASTER

when the thirty-second of Das inter-
sects the minus of Adze.

Zogg (ZOGG!)
The last world.